P9-CKX-609

KAY THOMPSON'S ELOISE

Eloise and the Very Secret Room

STORY BY Ellen Weiss
ILLUSTRATED BY Tammie Lyon

READY-TO-READ

SIMON SPOTLIGHT
NEW YORK LONDON TORONTO SYDNEY

ABDOPUBLISHING.COM

Reinforced library bound edition published in 2016 by Spotlight,
a division of ABDO, PO Box 398166, Minneapolis, Minnesota 55439.
Spotlight produces high-quality reinforced library bound editions for
schools and libraries. Published by agreement with Simon Spotlight.

Printed in the United States of America, North Mankato, Minnesota.
042015
092015

SIMON SPOTLIGHT
An imprint of Simon & Schuster Children's Publishing Division
1230 Avenue of the Americas, New York, NY 10020

LIBRARY OF CONGRESS CATALOGING-IN-PUBLICATION DATA

This title was previously cataloged with the following information:

Weiss, Ellen, 1949–
Eloise and the very secret room / story by Ellen Weiss ; illustrated by Tammie Lyon.—
1st Aladdin Paperbacks ed.
p. cm.— (Kay Thompson's Eloise) (Ready-to-read)
"Based on the art of Hilary Knight"—P. [1] of cover.
Summary: Eloise discovers the Plaza Hotel's Lost and Found
and decides to make it her secret playroom.
ISBN-13: 978-0-689-87450-5 (pbk)
ISBN-10: 0-689-87450-2 (pbk)
[1. Lost and found possessions—Fiction. 2. Plaza Hotel (New York, N.Y.)—Fiction.
3. Hotels, motels, etc.—Fiction. 4. Humorous stories.] I. Lyon, Tammie, ill.
II. Thompson, Kay, 1911– III. Knight, Hilary, ill. IV. Title. V. Series.
VI. Series: Ready-to-read.
PZ7.W4475Elo 2006
[E]—dc22

2005029648

978-1-61479-403-5 (reinforced library bound edition)

Spotlight
A Division of ABDO
abdopublishing.com

My name is Eloise.
I am six.

I live on
the tippy-top floor
of The Plaza Hotel.

But I can go all over.

This is Skipperdee.
He wears sneakers.
Sometimes.

Skipperdee and I
like to take walks.

Here is what I like to do:
go down that very, very,
long, long hall.

(It is the one that
goes past the room
with the stringy mops.)

There is a room
that is so secret
only I know about it.

Skipperdee and I, anyway.

It says LOST AND FOUND.

Maybe it is lost,
but I found it.

There are very good things in it.

If you tie a lot of
ties together,
you can jump rope.

It is also a good room
to spin in.

If we get tired,
we take a nap on a
fur coat.

Here is what else I can do:
wear nineteen hats.

A tennis racket makes
a very good turtle carrier.

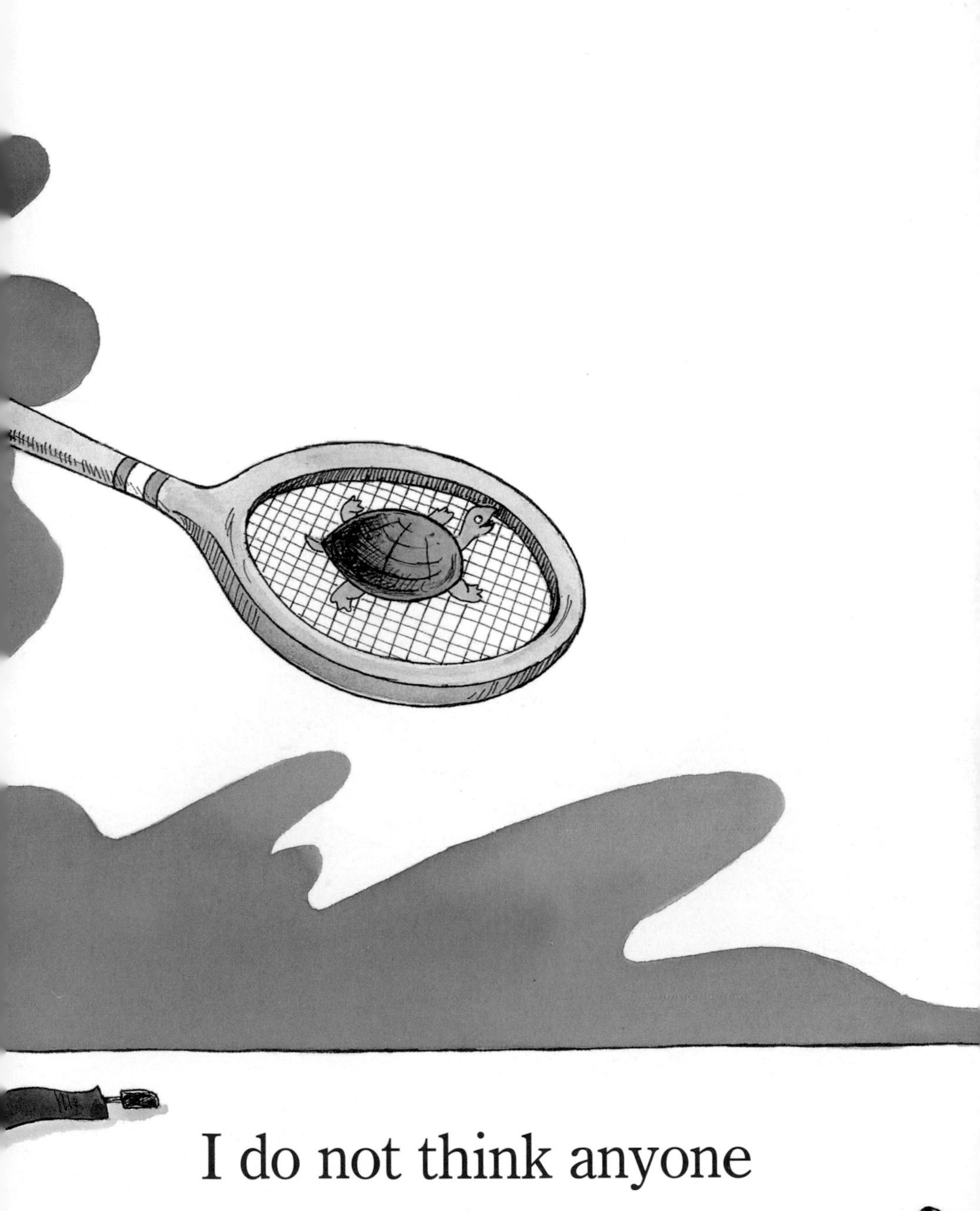

I do not think anyone
has ever been in
this room but me.

It is a good room
to practice hollering in.

A hatbox makes a very good drum.

In comes Nanny.
“Eloise!” she says.
“Here you are!”

In comes the manager.
"Eloise!" he says.
"Here you are!"

"Of course I am here,"
I say.
"Where else would I be?"

“We found you
in the Lost and Found,”
says Nanny.

I was not lost at all.
I was right here
all the time.
Oooooooo I love, love, love
the Lost and Found.

Tomorrow I will see if that hat makes a good fishbowl.